SUPER-INCREDIBLE ANIMALS

12 SUPER-FAST ANIMALS YOU NEED TO KNOW

by Tammy Gagne

12 STORY LIBRARY

www.12StoryLibrary.com

12-Story Library is an imprint of Bookstaves.

Produced for 12-Story Library by Red Line Editorial

Photographs ©: GP232/iStockphoto, cover, 1, 10; jacotakepics/Shutterstock Images, 4; gribben/iStockphoto, 5; Bildagentur Zoonar GmbH/Shutterstock Images, 6; Humpata/iStockphoto, 7; bikeriderlondon/Shutterstock Images, 8, 28; Volodymyr Burdiak/Shutterstock Images, 9; Stuart G. Porter/Shutterstock Images, 11; yanikap/Shutterstock Images, 12; kayjummac/iStockphoto, 13, 29; ACEgan/Shutterstock Images, 14; Herve06/iStockphoto, 15; Jim H. Walling/Shutterstock Images, 16; olikim/iStockphoto, 17; Frank Hildebrand/iStockphoto, 18; Missing35mm/iStockphoto, 19; Dennis Donohue/iStockphoto, 20; rpbirdman/iStockphoto, 21; Darren Pearson/iStock/Thinkstock, 22; holbox/Shutterstock Images, 23; Bryan Toro/iStockphoto, 24; Bonish Photography/iStockphoto, 25; Ivan Kuzmin/Shutterstock Images, 26; Tomatito/Shutterstock Images, 27

ISBN
978-1-63235-137-1 (hardcover)
978-1-63235-179-1 (paperback)
978-1-62143-231-9 (hosted ebook)

Library of Congress Control Number: 2015934275

Printed in the United States of America
Mankato, MN
June, 2015

TABLE OF CONTENTS

1

AMERICAN QUARTER HORSES RACE DOWN THE TRACK

People race horses for a reason. These large creatures are amazingly fast. Some are faster than others, however. The American quarter horse is the fastest breed for short distances. It can run 0.25 miles (0.4 km) in less than 21 seconds.

In addition to track races, people also use quarter horses in rodeos. A fast horse makes easy work of racing around the barrels. It also helps a rider catch a calf before tying its legs with rope. Quarter horses are also a popular choice for leisurely riding. Some quarter horses even appear in movies about the Old West.

There are 17 recognized coat colors of the American quarter horse.

The first quarter horses date back to the 1660s. Great Britain shipped tame horses to the British colonies in North America. Colonists then bred these horses with Spanish horses. The result was the animal we know today. In 1940, fans of these horses formed a registry. This list included many details about the new breed. Owners use it to make sure they breed horses with the best possible traits.

A woman competes with her American quarter horse in a pole bending competition.

2.5 million
Number of quarter horses registered by the late 1900s.

- The quarter horse is one of the oldest horse breeds in the United States.
- Quarter horses are known for their calm nature.
- A quarter horse weighs 950 to 1,200 pounds (431 to 544 kg).

A DIFFERENT KIND OF RACE

Quarter horses used on ranches must be fast in many ways. Life on a ranch does not involve track racing. But these horses must be able to run, turn, and stop quickly. All of these skills are important for separating a single cow from a herd.

2

BLUE WILDEBEEST JOIN THE STAMPEDE

The blue wildebeest lives on the grassy plains of eastern and southern Africa. This large species shares the savanna with many dangerous creatures. Some, such as lions and hyenas, are known for their speed. Fortunately, the blue wildebeest is also super-fast. It can run at speeds around 50 miles per hour (80 km/h). This usually gives the animal a fair chance of escape.

Blue wildebeest are a type of antelope. They live in large groups.

Blue wildebeest have a long black mane and beard.

Some blue wildebeest travel as many as 30 miles (48 km) in a single day.

When one senses a nearby predator such as a lion, it will warn the others with special grunts. The entire group then begins to run. This thunderous event is called a stampede.

Wildebeest can also sense when rain is coming. They move toward the areas where the storms are taking place. Land that receives rain usually has plenty of grass for the wildebeest to eat.

10,000
Size of an average wildebeest herd.

- The blue wildebeest is also known as the brindled gnu.
- Wildebeest spend most of their lives roaming together in search of food and water.
- The entire herd will swim across rivers and lakes as they move from one place to another.

3

BROWN HARES OUTRUN PREDATORS

Hares move so quickly that one became the star of a well-known fable. People have been telling Aesop's story of the tortoise and the hare for decades. It begins with the hare bragging about his impressive speed to the much slower animal.

Brown hares are incredibly fast. They can move up to 47 miles per hour (76 km/h). That comes out to about 37 body lengths per second! This speed helps the animals escape many types of danger. Many animals are fiercer than hares. But hares can usually outrun these other creatures.

Hares look a lot like rabbits. But hares are bigger and have longer ears. They also stand more upright and run much faster than rabbits.

Brown hares will stand upright to fight another hare.

4

Approximate number of hares in a single litter.

- Female hares may give birth to three litters in one year.
- Young hares are called leverets.
- Unlike rabbits, hares are not kept as pets.
- A group of hares is called a drove.

SPEED MEETS STRENGTH

When looking for mates in the spring, male hares chase after females. But sometimes a female hare does not want the male's attention. When this happens, the female has a unique way of showing him she is not interested. She stands upright and strikes the male with her front paws. This is called boxing.

Brown hares stretch their bodies out as they run.

4

CHEETAHS ARE BUILT TO RUN

The cheetah's body helps this big cat reach speeds up to 61 miles per hour (98 km/h). The animal has a very flexible spine. This allows the cheetah's front legs to stretch farther forward. When the cheetah is running, its claws act similar to cleats. Even the animal's tail plays a part. It acts like a rudder, helping the cheetah turn without losing speed.

Cheetahs do not just reach the same speeds as automobiles. They can also accelerate quickly like cars do. When they start off running, cheetahs can increase their speed up to four times more quickly than human runners can. And unlike most cars, cheetahs

Cheetahs can run fast from a young age.

Cheetahs use their speed for catching super-fast prey.

4

Number of days a cheetah can go without drinking water.

- Unlike other big cats, cheetahs usually hunt during the day.
- Cheetahs have excellent eyesight.
- In addition to running fast, cheetahs can also turn quickly.
- When a cheetah hunts prey, the chase is usually over in less than one minute.

THINK ABOUT IT

Cheetahs look like they are built for speed. Based on what you have read in this section, which traits do you think help the cheetah most in running fast?

can also stop quickly. As fast as they can move, cheetahs cannot keep up their super-fast speed for long distances. They can usually do it long enough to catch other animals, though.

CHEETAHS SPEED UP QUICKLY

Few animals can beat the cheetah's speed record. And in the past decade, the cheetah has been beating its own record. In 2001, a cheetah named Nyana set a record of 6.19 seconds for 328 feet (100 m). Nyana was born through the Cheetah Outreach program. This organization breeds cheetahs to keep them from becoming an endangered species. In 2009, a cheetah named Sarah set a new record of 6.13 seconds for the same distance. Three years later, Sarah went for yet another record run. This time she finished the run in 5.95 seconds!

5

DRAGONFLIES ZOOM THROUGH THE AIR

Dragonflies are the fastest flying insects. Dragonfly wings move so fast that the human eye cannot actually see them beating. They are a blur to people as a dragonfly zooms past.

Dragonflies have two sets of wings. They help make the insect a fast and strong flier. Dragonflies can fly forward and backward. They can also change direction in midair. Dragonflies can even hover in the air for up to one minute.

Dragonflies can fly up to 35 miles per hour (56 km/h).

There are nearly 6,000 species of dragonflies around the world.

3.5

Average length, in inches (8.9 cm), of a dragonfly's wingspan.

- Prehistoric dragonflies had wings that measured two feet (0.61 m).
- Dragonflies only eat prey they catch while flying. If they lose the ability to fly, dragonflies will starve to death.
- A single dragonfly can eat hundreds of mosquitoes in just one day.

Dragonflies use their speed when hunting for food. They are among the top predators of the insect world. They will eat almost any other bug they can catch. Dragonflies grab their prey out of the air with their feet.

Dragonflies have lived on earth for approximately 300 million years. Today thousands of dragonfly species exist all over the world. They come in a large variety of colors and patterns.

6

LEATHERBACK SEA TURTLES GLIDE UNDERWATER

Few turtles are known for their speed. The leatherback sea turtle, however, is one of the fastest animals in the water. It can swim at speeds of up to 15 miles per hour (24 km/h). Even the fastest humans can only swim 4.7 miles per hour (7.6 km/h).

Leatherback turtles are the largest turtle species in the world. They are also different from other turtles in

Small fish help keep a leatherback sea turtle's shell clean.

2,000
Weight, in pounds (907 kg), of a leatherback sea turtle.

- Leatherbacks can stay in deep water for up to 85 minutes.
- The temperature of the nest determines whether turtles will hatch male or female.
- Although scientists study leatherback turtles, no one knows exactly how long they live.

several ways. Other turtle species have hard shells. The leatherback's shell is softer and more flexible. It helps the animal move more easily through the water. The leatherback's long flippers act similar to paddles.

AN ALL-AROUND ATHLETE

The leatherback turtle is not just fast. It can also cover great distances. Members of this species have been known to swim up to 3,000 miles (4,828 km). They have also been seen diving to depths of 3,281 feet (1,000 m).

Leatherback sea turtles live in more parts of the world than any other species. They can be found as far north as Norway and as far south as New Zealand. A thick layer of body fat keeps the turtle warm even in cold water.

Hatchlings must quickly make their way to the ocean after being born.

7

MITES ARE SPEEDY LITTLE CREATURES

A recent study revealed that the fastest land animal is the mite. This tiny creature is no bigger than a sesame seed. The mite can move 322 times its own body length in a single second. Scientists explain that this accomplishment is similar to a human running 1,300 miles per hour (2,092 km/h).

Mites are arachnids that were first discovered in 1916. Scientists know

There are many different types of mites.

THINK ABOUT IT

Mites certainly move fast compared to their body size. Considering the greater distances that other fast animals from this book cover, do you think the mite should indeed be named the fastest animal?

little about them even after one century. Researchers have observed mites on sunny concrete as hot as 140 degrees Fahrenheit (60 °C). Temperatures this high typically kill other animals.

Little is known about the life cycle of this tiny creature. Both its speed and size make studying the mite a challenge. A person cannot see some mites' legs without a magnifying glass. Scientists think mites move so fast to catch prey. So far, though, they have not been able to identify the prey, because it is too small.

0.1

Length, in inches (0.25 cm), of the *Paratarsotomus macropalpis* mite.

- This super-fast mite species is found in southern California.
- It was first identified in 1916.
- This mite is often found running across rocks or sidewalks.

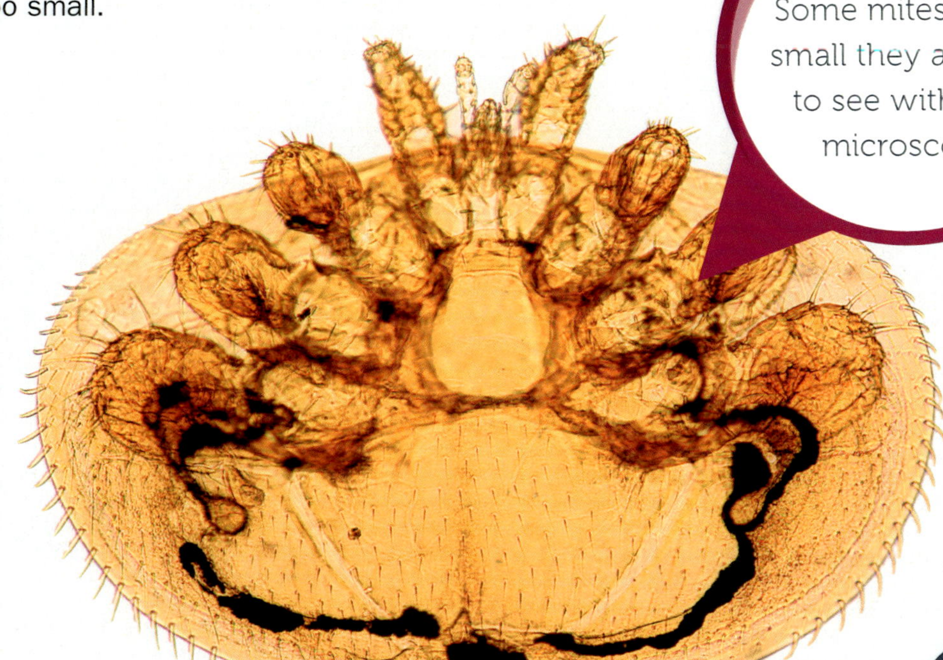

8

PEREGRINE FALCONS DIVE FOR PREY

The peregrine falcon can fly as fast as 69 miles per hour (111 km/h). This speed alone is impressive. But when this animal dives after prey, it moves even faster. A peregrine falcon dropping through the air can move 200 miles per hour (322 km/h).

The biggest part of the peregrine falcon's diet is other birds. The falcon will dive after them in the air. When this determined predator is diving, it moves as fast as a professional racecar. To reach its

Peregrine falcons can live up to 17 years in the wild.

top speed, the peregrine falcon must first reach spectacular heights. When it starts diving, it can be 0.62 miles (1 km) above the ground.

Peregrine falcons are found on all of the world's continents except Antarctica. They were listed as an endangered species for many years. But the falcon was removed from the list in 1999.

Peregrine falcons sit on high perches to watch for prey below.

1,650

Approximate number of peregrine falcon pairs living in the United States and Canada.

- The peregrine falcon's name comes from the Latin word *peregrinus*, which means "to wander."
- It is also called the duck hawk.
- The peregrine falcon has a hooked beak for catching prey.
- Peregrine falcons mate for life.

MATING AND NESTING

Male peregrine falcons use their flying skills to attract mates. They show off for females during mating season. Flying high means peregrine falcons can make their homes in some lofty spots. Their nests have been found high on bridges, cliffs, and even skyscrapers.

9

PRONGHORN ANTELOPE OUTRUN THEIR PREDATORS

Pronghorn antelope are the fastest North American land animal. These swift creatures move nearly 60 miles per hour (97 km/h). That is the same speed that cars drive on the highway!

Pronghorn antelope are so fast that they can outrun most of their predators. How then do they even have predators? Animals such as bobcats and coyotes have learned they must corner the antelope.

These super-fast creatures are not just good for short bursts of energy. They can

If there is any escape route, a pronghorn antelope will get away.

3

Height, in feet (0.91 m), of a pronghorn antelope from hoof to shoulder.

- They are named for their curved horns, which can be one foot (0.3 m) long.
- Pronghorn antelope can travel for miles at half their top speed.
- When this species senses danger, it will raise the fur on its backside. This exposes a white patch of fur that warns the other members of the herd.
- A pronghorn antelope that is only a few days old can outrun a human being.

Pronghorn antelope have great eyesight and can see predators from far away.

also keep up their high speed longer than many other species can. A cheetah would probably beat the antelope in a 100-yard (90-m) dash. The antelope would be the winner, though, in a one-mile (1.6-km) race. This trait helps pronghorn antelope escape fiercer animals.

10

SAILFISH JUMP THROUGH THE WAVES

Imagine the fastest Olympic swimmer is racing against a sailfish in the 200-meter freestyle event. It would take this gifted human swimmer a little less than a minute and a half to complete the race. But the sailfish would be done in less than 10 seconds.

One thing that makes the sailfish so fast is its jumping ability. This species leaps out of the water while swimming.

Out of all the fish in the sea, the sailfish is

When a sailfish jumps, it moves even faster than it does in the water.

the fastest. This species can reach speeds of up to 68 miles per hour (109 km/h). Sailfish are not just the fastest fish. They are also one of the biggest saltwater fish. A large sailfish can measure up to 11 feet (3.4 m) long and weigh up to 220 pounds (100 kg).

Some people fish for the speedy sailfish.

36

Time, in hours, it takes for sailfish eggs to hatch once laid.

- A sailfish's upper jaw extends beyond its lower jaw, making it look like a spear.
- Sailfish are usually found close to the ocean's surface.
- A sailfish's diet consists of squid and octopus, among other foods.
- Few people eat sailfish, as their meat is tough.

CATCHING THE SAILFISH

The sailfish is a popular species for sport fishing. Many want to catch this super-fast animal. But it can take hours to catch a sailfish. The sailfish's size makes catching one very difficult. Once hooked, a sailfish will fight intensely. It may leap and dive, trying its hardest to break free.

11

SHORTFIN MAKO SHARKS LEAP OUT OF THE WATER

The shortfin mako is the fastest shark species in the world. It swims quickly both in short bursts and over longer periods of time. Many shortfin makos swim approximately 22 miles per hour (35 km/h). Some move even faster.

This species holds a speed record for long-distance travel. Researchers have found that shortfin makos can swim 1,320 miles (2,124 km) in 37 days. That means this species can swim approximately 36 miles (58 km) in a single day!

Shortfin makos are not just known for their speed. Many people also

Shortfin mako sharks can swim quickly through the water.

THINK ABOUT IT

The shortfin mako shark is fast in two different ways. Find one or two sentences in the main text section to support this point.

admire this sea creature's jumping ability. The species often leaps up to 20 feet (6.1 m) out of the water when hunting sea birds or flying fish.

43

Speed, in miles per hour (69 km/h), of the fastest shortfin mako on record.

- The shortfin mako is the fastest of all sharks.
- This species also has excellent speed over long distances.
- Shortfin makos can jump 20 feet (6.1 m) into the air.
- They may even jump into boats when hooked, injuring people in the process.

Some shortfin makos jump into fishing boats when hooked.

12

WIND SCORPIONS SCURRY THROUGH THE SAND

The wind scorpion is among the world's fastest land animals. The 10 miles per hour (16 km/h) it runs may not seem very fast at first. But consider this animal's size. The wind scorpion can cover a distance of several times its own body length in a single second!

Some people tell wild stories about wind scorpions. One myth states that this species screams. The truth is that very few wind scorpions make any sound at all. Another myth claims that these tiny creatures chase human beings. Some wind scorpions do in fact run toward people. But they are likely following the humans' shadows. This species prefers shade to sunlight.

The wind scorpion is also called the camel spider. But it is actually neither a scorpion nor a spider. Instead, it is classified as an arachnid. These eight-legged creatures are known for their speed.

Most wind scorpions are less than two inches (5.1 cm) long.

5

Length, in inches (13 cm), of a wind scorpion's leg span.

- Wind scorpions have hairy bodies.
- They will attack rodents, lizards, and even small birds.
- A wind scorpion's jaw can extend as far as a third of its body length.
- Wind scorpions are not poisonous. They can, however, deliver a painful bite to humans.

Wind scorpions live in deserts of the Middle East, the southwestern United States, and Mexico.

FACT SHEET

- Many super-fast animals, such as cheetahs, use their speed for catching prey. Other animals, such as the pronghorn antelope, rely on their swiftness for fleeing from predators. Some animals do both. A hyena can kill a young cheetah cub—unless it can escape.

- Legs play a big part in the speed of land animals. The brown hare's strong hind legs help it jump up to 10 feet (3 m) at a time. The cheetah's long legs help it make the most of each step. This super-fast animal moves 20 to 22 feet (6.1 to 6.7 m) with each stride while running.

- Like the brown hare, a big part of the sailfish's speed comes from jumping. As the sailfish leaves the water, its large dorsal fin lies close to its body. Doing so helps the animal move faster. With the fin up, the wind could slow the fish down.

- You have probably heard that there is strength in numbers. This saying is certainly true for some of the fastest animals. Lions will attack a single wildebeest if they can catch it. They will not go after a herd, however. A single stampede could kill the lions.

- Being fast is not always a guarantee of survival. A female leatherback sea turtle can lay up to 150 eggs at a time. Only a few of the turtles from these eggs will reach adulthood, however. Sharks, other fish, and even sea birds eat young sea turtles.
- Wind scorpions are not just fast. They are also aggressive—even with each other. During World War I, soldiers in Egypt would catch wind scorpions and stage fights between them. The men would bet on which animals would win the battles.

GLOSSARY

accelerate
To move or cause to move faster.

arachnid
An animal having a segmented body divided into two regions of which the front part bears four pairs of legs but no antennae.

endangered
Threatened with extinction.

flexible
Capable of being bent.

hover
To hang fluttering in the air.

predator
An animal that preys on others for food.

rudder
A flat movable piece attached to the rear of a ship or aircraft for steering.

savanna
A grassland containing scattered trees.

stampede
A wild rush or flight of frightened animals.

FOR MORE INFORMATION

Books

Ipcizade, Catherine. *The Fastest Animals*. Mankato, MN: Capstone Press, 2011.

Spelman, Lucy. *National Geographic Animal Encyclopedia*. Washington, DC: National Geographic Children's Books, 2012.

Stewart, Melissa. *World's Fastest Animals*. New York: Sterling Children's Books, 2014.

Websites

Conservation Institute: Fastest Animals on Earth
www.conservationinstitute.org/10-fastest-animals-on-earth

Florida Museum of National History: Shortfin Mako Sharks
www.flmnh.ufl.edu/fish/gallery/descript/shortfinmako/shortfinmako.html

National Geographic: Leatherback Sea Turtles
animals.nationalgeographic.com/animals/reptiles/leatherback-sea-turtle

INDEX

About the Author

Tammy Gagne has written more than 100 books for adults and children. She resides in northern New England with her husband and son. One of her favorite pastimes is visiting schools to talk to children about the writing process.